Be Nice. Be Kind.

Be Nice. Be Kind. Be Great.

Juris P. Prudence's Holiday Gift

J.N. Childress

Be Nice. Be Kind. Be Great.

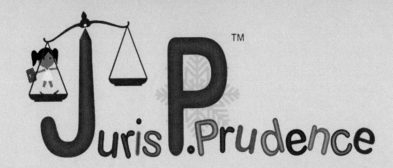

ISBN-13: 978-1-946456-05-2
ISBN-10: 1-946456-05-5

Printed in the USA.

Juris Prudence LLC
www.jurispprudence.com

To Dan Westman-

Thank you for being an exemplar of integrity, civility, and kindness. You not only taught me the nuts and bolts of practicing law, but you also taught me how to practice with kindness. It was a true honor to be your colleague.

-JNC

It was the most wonderful time of the year. The holiday season had arrived! Juris P. Prudence patiently waited for this season to arrive every year.

J.P. loved celebrating all of the holidays that took place in December! This year was a bit different from holidays in past years. People were not being as friendly to each other this year. They were being really mean! All of this meanness made J.P. very sad.

"You're stupid, Ms. Johnson! I can't believe you think that way." Ms. Coleman shouted, waiving her fist in the air at another passenger on the metro train. The metro was the train that J.P. rode to school on days that she did not ride her bike to school. The metro traveled all around the District of Columbia, the city where J.P. lived.

"Move out of the way! I have to get to work!" A woman in a green and yellow shirt shouted at J.P. as she got off of the metro train.

Shocked by all of the mean people she had just seen on the train, J.P. left the train station and headed to her law school at the National Kids Leaders Academy. Ms. Nicholson was her first teacher of the day.

"Good morning, young lawyers! Your holiday break starts tomorrow. During the holidays, your assignment is to study chapter three in your contracts book. As you know, a contract is a promise between two or more people, a promisor and a promisee. A contract creates a responsibility between those people. Your assignment is to find a way to use contracts to help people. You may work with your friends on this assignment," Ms. Nicholson instructed the class.

The school day went on, and J.P. went to lunch, meeting her best friends, Maddy, Sofie, and Izzy. Even though they were all only eleven-years-old, they were all lawyers. "What are you guys doing for the holiday break?" J.P. asked.

"I'll be home with my family! I hope it snows!" Izzy stated happily.

"I'm excited about our class project! I love contracts! It's my favorite legal subject!" Sofie exclaimed.

During lunch, J.P. overheard some of her classmates talking loudly. "You're not cool enough to sit here, new kid!" James shouted at Trent. Trent sadly left James' table and went to sit alone at another table.

J.P. heard what James had said and walked over to Trent. "You can sit with me and my friends," J.P. guided Trent to her table.

"Oh cool! I'm Trent."

"I'm Juris, but people call me J.P. for short. These are my best friends, Sofie, Maddy, and Izzy. We're all in the law program at K.L.A."

"I'm in the engineering program here. My family just moved to D.C. I'm from a small town in North Carolina. It's been really hard to make new friends since I moved. Thanks for letting me sit with you."

Trent, Maddy, Sofie, Izzy, and J.P. ate their lunches together and talked about their plans for the holidays.

The school day ended, and the holiday break had officially begun! J.P. rushed home to tell her grandmother all about her day at school. "Granny, I have to use contracts to help people!"

"Oh my, honey! That's a big task. There's so much trouble in the world. We could sure use anything to make the world a better place," Granny stated.

It was getting late, and it was time for J.P. to get ready for bed. Before she went to bed, she was going to read chapter three on contracts in her textbook, just like Ms. Nicholson had assigned.

"A CONTRACT IS A PROMISE BETWEEN TWO OR MORE PEOPLE. A CONTRACT CREATES A RESPONSIBILITY BETWEEN THOSE PEOPLE. THE PROMISOR IS THE PERSON MAKING THE PROMISE. THE PROMISEE IS THE PERSON ACCEPTING THE PROMISE. THE PROMISOR MAKES THE PROMISE TO THE PROMISEE."

J.P. repeated the words that she had just read, "A contract is a promise!" A light bulb went off in her head. "What if contracts could be used to create promises between people to be nice to one another?" she thought to herself. "Aha! I'll create kindness contracts! That is how I will use contracts to help people! These contracts will be my gift to the community for Christmas Day!" J.P. determined.

J.P. woke up early the next day. It was Christmas Eve, but J.P. had work to do! She called Izzy, Maddy, and Sofie to tell them about her idea for kindness contracts. They all loved the idea! The girls met in the library that morning to start drafting the kindness contracts that they would ask promisors to sign.

J.P. and her friends decided on the people they would ask to sign kindness contracts. There was a special group of people that J.P. wanted to sign these contracts.

Kindness Contracts List

1. James would not let Trent sit at table.

2. Ms. Coleman called Ms. Jamison a mean name.

3. Lady in yellow and green shirt on the metro yelled at me.

J.P.'s first person to find was James. Luckily, James lived in her neighborhood. She walked to his house and knocked on his door.

"Hey, J.P.! It's snowing outside. What are you doing out in the cold?" James asked.

"Hi, James. Yesterday at school, I noticed that you didn't let Trent sit at the table with you. That wasn't cool."

"I'm sorry, J.P. I realized that I was being mean. Some of my friends were making fun of Trent for being the new kid at school, and they told me not to let him sit at our table. I was wrong for being a bully. I won't do it again."

"Yes, you and your friends were wrong for the way you treated Trent. How would you feel if our classmates didn't let you sit at their table?"

"I'd feel really sad." James responded.

"I'm asking you to sign a kindness contract. In the contract, you have to promise to apologize to Trent for not letting him sit at your table. You also have to ask your friends to apologize. And, you have to let Trent sit at your table from now on. Deal?"

"Deal. Where do I sign?" James asked.

"You sign where it says, 'promisor.' You're the promisor because you're the person making a promise to me. I'm the promisee because I'm accepting your promise." J.P. responded.

James signed the kindness contract.

"I'm giving you a kindness band for signing the contract. Put your band on your wrist. Always remember what it says."

James read his band. "Be nice. Be kind. Be great."

The snow was piling up on the ground, but J.P. had more work to do. Ms. Coleman was next on her list of people to find. Ms. Coleman had called Ms. Jamison a mean name on the metro train. Ms. Coleman lived in J.P.'s neighborhood, so J.P. did not have to walk far to get to her house. J.P. knew her well because she had helped Ms. Coleman deliver clothes to a local charity last year.

J.P. knocked on the door, and Ms. Coleman answered. "Hi, Juris!" Ms. Coleman greeted J.P. with a shocked look on her face. "What are you doing here? It's Christmas Eve! You should be at home with your family. Come inside. It's cold out."

"Hi, Ms. Coleman. On the metro yesterday, you did something that really disappointed me."

"What did I do, Juris?"

"You called Ms. Jamison, 'stupid' because she didn't agree with your opinion. Everyone's opinion matters. You shouldn't call people names just because they don't agree with you."

Be Nice. Be Kind. Be Great.

"Juris, oh my. I'm so embarrassed, and I'm really sorry." Ms. Coleman's eyes filled with tears.

"I forgive you. I am asking that you promise to respect everyone's opinion and not call people names for disagreeing with you. Would you sign a kindness contract making this promise?"

"Give me that contract, Juris! I'll sign right now!" J.P. handed Ms. Coleman a kindness contract and a kindness band.

"Remember what your band says, Ms. Coleman. It will remind you to always be nice."

J.P. left Ms. Coleman's house to find the last person on her kindness contract list, the woman in the yellow and green tee shirt. There was one problem. She didn't know her name, and she didn't know where she lived or worked. How would J.P. find her?

J.P. had one clue. She had seen the yellow and green tee shirts that the woman was wearing before, but where? She thought carefully, but she could not remember where she had seen those tee shirts before.

The snow was coming down as J.P. walked around the city, searching cafes, restaurants, and office buildings, looking for the woman in the yellow and green tee shirt. Today was Christmas Eve. J.P. had to have her kindness contracts signed by Christmas Day. This was J.P.'s gift to her community for Christmas Day!

J.P. called her friends and asked them to meet her at the police station. Maybe Officer Valdez could help find the lady in the green and yellow tee shirt.

Be Nice. Be Kind. Be Great.

"Hi, J.P., Maddy, Sofie, and Izzy! What brings you young ladies to the police station on Christmas Eve? Is everything okay?" Officer Valdez asked.

"Hi Officer Valdez! I need your help. I'm looking for a lady who was mean to me on the metro train. I'm trying to give a gift to my community by Christmas Day. My gift is to ask people to sign contracts promising to be nice. I really want to ask the lady I saw on the metro to sign my kindness contract."

"Officer Valdez, can you give us some tips to help find this lady?" Izzy asked.

"I commend you girls for always trying to make the world a better place. Don't give up your search. Magical things happen during the holiday season. But, it's getting late. You should go home. It will be getting dark soon, and the weather is getting worse. I'm sure your families want you home soon."

"You're right, Officer Valdez. We better go, you guys! Every Christmas Eve, my family serves dinner to homeless families. I can't be late!"

""Juris Providence Prudence! Where have you been? We have to leave for the shelter in just a little while. Come taste the Louisiana gumbo I've been working on all day. I can't get your grandfather away from it!" Granny stated. "How do you like it?"

"It's great, Granny! I love it!" J.P. responded.

"I love it too!" Granddaddy chimed in.

"We know you love it! You've been eating it all day!" Granny laughed. "Come on, y'all! John, you pack up that gumbo, and y'all both go put your coats on. We need to be at the shelter by six o'clock, and we don't want to be late!" Granny ordered.

"Granny, I still haven't found the last person to sign my kindness contract. I've been looking for her all afternoon."

"Well, honey, you've done your best. And you never know. The day is not over, but now, we must hurry and get to the shelter."

J.P. looked forward to serving dinner at the homeless shelter every Christmas Eve. She couldn't wait to serve Granny's famous gumbo this year and meet the families at the shelter. But, one thing was bothering her.

She still wanted to find the woman in the green and yellow tee shirt before Christmas day. She remembered what Officer Valdez said earlier, "Magical things happen during the holiday season."

"Merry Christmas, Prudence Family!" Mr. Miles greeted J.P. and her grandparents. He managed the shelter and organized the Christmas Eve dinner every year. J.P.'s mouth dropped open when she saw him.

"Something wrong, J.P.?"

"No, it's just your shirt! Now, I remember how I know those shirts! They are the staff shirts for people who work at the shelter!"

"What do you mean, Juris?" **Mr. Miles** was confused.

"On the metro yesterday, there was a lady wearing the same green and yellow shirt you are wearing now. She yelled at me, and it hurt my feelings. I have been looking for her all day. I want to ask her to sign a kindness contract. I've gotten two other people to sign today. These contracts are my **Christmas** gifts to the community. When people are nice to each other, the community is stronger." J.P. explained.

"What a wonderful gift, Juris. That is so thoughtful. We have a very small staff here. There's **Mr. Martinez, Ms. Abby,** and **Ms. Cohen.** Here's a picture of our staff." **Mr. Miles** pulled out his phone and showed J.P. a picture.

"That's her! That's the woman I saw on the metro!" J.P. pointed at the picture.

"That's **Ms. Abby.** She's standing over there. Let me introduce you to her."

"So nice to meet you, Juris! You look very familiar." Ms. Abby smiled.

"Hi Ms. Abby. I'm so happy to meet you again! I've actually been looking for you all day. You ride the same metro train as I do to get to school. You were on the metro yesterday. You yelled at me when you were getting off of the train."

"I'm so sorry, Juris! I had no idea. I've been so busy working at the shelter this week. It's no excuse, but I was rushing to the shelter yesterday and wasn't paying attention to what I was saying or to my tone of voice."

"Will you sign a kindness contract, promising to always use kind words, even when you're rushing or busy?" J.P. handed Ms. Abby the kindness contract.

"Absolutely! I'll sign right now!"

J.P. had all of her kindness contracts signed. She had given her community the gift of kindness, and she felt great! After eating Granny's gumbo with families at the shelter, she returned home that night with a full stomach and a full heart.

The next morning, Christmas Day had come. J.P., Izzy, Maddy, and Sofie had a tradition of exchanging gifts at J.P.'s house.

"Under the tree, there's a gift waiting for you girls. It arrived on our doorstep this morning, but we don't know who sent it. It has all of your names on it." Granny told J.P. and her friends.

The girls gathered beside the Christmas tree, filled with excitement over their surprise gift. They unwrapped the gift together. When they opened it, they couldn't believe their eyes.

They pulled a huge framed certificate out of the wrapped gift box, which read:

To Juris, Izzy, Maddy, and Sofie: Thank you for using the law to do great things for our community. You are a gift to the people of the District of Columbia. Sincerely, the Mayor of Washington, D.C.

"This is so cool!" Maddy exclaimed.

"Yes, this is really awesome, but do you know what the best gift of all is?" J.P. asked her friends.

"What's that, J.P?" Izzy responded.

"The best gift of all is the gift of being nice, being kind, and being great."

THE END

Juris P. Prudence CONTRACT

I promise to be kind to everyone I meet. I will carry out this promise by doing the following:

_____

_____

_____

_____

_____

_____

_____

_____

This contract is made on _____ (date)

between _____ (promisor)

and _____ (promisee).

Be Kind!

Do you want more kindness contracts? Purchase *Juris P. Prudence's Kindness Contracts* on Amazon.com and on www.jurispprudence.com!

Visit www.jurispprudence.com to get all of the fun and educational products in the Juris P. Prudence Collection!*

*You must be 13 years-old or older to sign up for the Juris P. Prudence newsletter.

Made in the USA
San Bernardino, CA
09 December 2019